SILVERWING

by Kenneth Steven

Illustrated by Ishy Walters

Neem Tree
PRESS

Published by Neem Tree Press Limited 2021
info@neemtreepress.com

Neem Tree Press Limited,
95A Ridgmount Gardens, London, WC1E 7AZ

Text Copyright © Kenneth Steven 2021
Cover Design and Illustrations Copyright © Isaebel Walters 2021

A catalogue record for this book is available from the British Library

ISBN 978-1-911107-33-0 Paperback
ISBN 978-1-911107-34-7 Ebook

Printed and bound in Great Britain by
Biddles Limited

SILVERWING

by Kenneth Steven

Illustrated by Ishy Walters

NEEM TREE
PRESS

For Ali and Kirsty, with love, and to
remember your Mum.

Table of Contents

1

Douglas sat on the wooden chest that once had belonged to his mother and gazed out over the fields.

Everyone else hated that last bit of autumn. They moaned about it and wished for it to be over. Douglas, however, saw a beautiful, mysterious world. The fields were filled with shallow ditches of water that reflected the light grey sky. The far trees and low hills above them were almost invisible through the mist. Douglas could only just distinguish their outlines. It was true that everything was a different shade of grey, but it was not true that it was boring and miserable. This was the most magical bit of the entire year, when anything might happen. At night, the winds came and shook the skies, the woods and the house too. Sometimes Douglas woke and did not want to go back to sleep; he imagined he was in a great ship. His cabin rocked from side to side in the storm, buffeted by the gales.

'Can you get some coal?' his dad, John, asked.

He was pulled from his reverie. He turned around, but his dad had gone already, so he didn't answer. Douglas didn't want to go, but he knew he'd better all the same. He padded down the wooden stairs and put on his boots in the porch, picked up the bucket.

Outside, he recognised a familiar sound. His feet crunched the gravel to go round the side of the house. A single call, then others. He tilted his head right back and looked up at sky. It was the geese! They had come back!

Douglas knew these were migrant birds that left in the spring, spent the summer in Iceland, and returned before the winter snows fell there.

That night he heard them circling the house. Their cries sounded like rusty wheels and they drifted in and out of his dreams. The night wasn't stormy, that was why he could hear them clearly. He thought about their journey, the flight across the seas from Iceland, and how they came back to the same field, year after year.

*

Douglas's mother had not come back. She had been ill for two years with a disease called cancer. The doctors kept saying that she would get better, but she never did. She had died almost a year ago now, last November.

He had returned from the hospital that night with his dad. The drive had taken perhaps an hour. It had rained for a whole week and there were deep pools that almost flooded the road completely. It was a back road that could take you to the city hospital, but almost no cars used it nowadays. Douglas didn't remember seeing another vehicle the whole way home.

He had thought that the skies and the trees had cried for his mother; they had all cried, and these were their tears. This was what they had given in their sadness. The car was warm, but he wished he could have got out and walked into the woods, even in the pitch-black outside. He believed that there he would meet his mother. She would come towards him and everything would be all right, everything would be as it once was.

But they drove on, mile after mile through the strange darkness and the floods, and he felt enclosed in a cocoon, as though he was wrapped in wool and didn't even know if he could move his hands or his feet. And afterwards, he wasn't sure if he and his dad had spoken or not. He only remembered the darkness and the floods and the warm car, and it was as if he was not really there at all.

In the hospital, his mother had whispered '*Douglas,*' and he had reached out and held her for a long time. She was still his mum. Her voice was just the same. And her face was still beautiful. But illness had aged her.

At first, when she had told him she was unwell, she hadn't seemed different at all. How could she be dying then? That was why he had believed the doctors when they said she would get better; she had never looked ill for the whole first year. She used to love running with Douglas. He would always win, partly because she always started laughing.

But in the weeks before she went to hospital for the last time, it was difficult for her to even get up the stairs. He had believed they would find what was wrong and she would get back to her old self again, that everything would be all right again.

But then the doctors had stopped saying that. He wanted to believe just the same that one day he'd find her, as she had been before, out there in the woods. They'd run together and laugh again, and they'd go looking for the geese.

*

Douglas woke up early and knew he had to go outside. He wanted to look out for the geese after last night. The room was chilly, but that didn't matter. He slipped out of bed and got dressed, quietly opened the door and crept downstairs. He did not want his dad to know he was going out. He put on his boots and clicked the back door shut behind him. There wasn't a single sound in the world. The neighbours who lived in the houses on each side were still asleep: the curtains in their grey stone houses closed.

He walked down to the bottom of the long garden, past all the old apple trees, to the little stile that crossed the fence into the field. He liked moving quietly, feeling he could step so softly he disturbed nothing at all.

The geese were nestled in the long grass, some still asleep, others looking around with their golden-yellow eyes. They were called greylags and had grey feathers edged with white, orange beaks and oddly pink legs. It was hard to spot them in the fields since they were camouflaged so well in the haze of the early morning light. Douglas stood and watched them for a while. Then he took a path down the field. He felt the rain on his face, not really rain but more a mist of pearly drops, feathery soft against his skin; the year was still not cold. After a while, the quiet was broken by a strange noise from the long grass – a squabbling sound, like nothing he had heard before.

He went towards it quickly and saw a lump moving, rolling about in the long grass.

He ran over and saw it was a goose, a toppled-over goose. He crouched down and was very still so it wouldn't be afraid, but the bird continued to squabble, trying to get away. It was injured; one of its wings looked a little torn.

Perhaps it had fallen? He had to help it; that was the only thing he knew for sure. Without thinking, Douglas took off his jacket, wrapped it around the bird and lifted it up in his arms, carrying it back the way he had come. It was much bigger and heavier than he had imagined, and it snapped at his hands as often as it could. Douglas bit his lip because his hands hurt a lot, but kept going.

*

The old shed was stuffed with paint pots and cupboard doors and broken handles. A place for Douglas's dad to put things he was going to mend but never did. One of the windowpanes was cracked and had never been mended. It wasn't easy getting the door open with the goose stabbing at his hands. Douglas staggered in, kicking an empty paint pot.

In front of him was an old table covered with tubes of glue and cloths and broken dishes. Douglas swept the mess away while holding the goose tightly under his right arm, all the while leaning against the table for support. With a heavy grunt, he heaved the goose onto the table, still wrapped in his jacket.

At least now he could rescue his hands; they were red and raw and sore.

He peered around the dimly lit shed. Under a pile of broken baskets, he recognised the dog bed that had belonged to his dad as a boy. He had owned a spaniel called Teddy. They had never had another dog, but they had kept the basket. He stumbled forwards and reached out to move the broken baskets. More junk crunched under his left foot. He stretched a little further and caught hold of the edge of Teddy's basket. There was still a rough woollen rug inside.

There was nothing for it but to lift the goose again, this time to place it in the basket. He bit his lip. Another finger got nipped by the bird's fierce beak, but finally, the goose was in. Now it was lying on its good side. At least here it would be safe and warm. He'd leave the shed door open a crack; there was nothing precious in there. Everything was broken, even the goose. He would come back with food once he'd had time to work out what food would be best.

And then he heard the back door opening at the house.

'Douglas! Breakfast is in five minutes!'

2

Later that day he searched on the internet to find out what greylag geese ate – but it was frustrating. The internet wanted to tell him where greylag geese came from, where they flew to, how far they could fly at one stretch, and why they were called greylag – but he couldn't find any articles on what they ate.

But as he looked out of his window, sitting on his mum's old chest, watching the grey fields under the grey skies, it slowly dawned on him. The geese had nothing special to eat out there! The fields that had crops earlier in the year were now full of stubble. So, before it got dark, he sneaked back over the stile and run down towards the stream that snaked through the field. He picked a handful of pieces then ran back up to the shed and stepped inside. Douglas used one of the broken baskets lying around and filled it with bits of stubble for the goose. He went back inside the house and found a plastic bowl in his dad's bathroom and filled that with water. Douglas put the stubble and water down in Teddy's old basket and got just one peck from the goose. He knew exactly what he needed to find if he wanted to spare his hands – a pair of really tough gloves. Running back into the house again, Douglas spotted his dad's thick red gloves on the mantlepiece and grabbed them. He also found a little rug by the front door that they never seemed to use for anything. He could use it as a blanket for the goose!

The bird lay down on its side again, and he didn't know what more to do. Maybe it would eat once he had gone? Douglas hoped it wouldn't die. He stared at the silver markings on its wing tips, at how beautiful they were. And the wings weren't just grey, there was white there too. It was like people thinking autumn was just one colour without seeing the myriad of shades. He wished he could have told his mum about him rescuing the goose. Douglas would have brought her out to the shed as soon as he had settled the bird in the basket; he would have shown her his sore hands but tell her they didn't really bother him. Together they'd stand here and watch the goose.

But she wasn't here. It was getting dark, and he had to go, or his dad would get worried.

'Good night, goose,' he whispered. Then, leaving the door just a little open, he dashed up the garden to the house.

*

On Monday afternoon Douglas came home from school, threw his bag in a corner of his room, and charged downstairs to make some toast. He couldn't wait to find out how the goose was doing. John came in with a cup of tea and sat down on the sofa.

'Douglas, d'you know where my new gloves are? The ones I got from your Aunt Helen? I can't find them anywhere.'

Douglas shook his head as heat rose in his cheeks.

'And d'you happen to know what's become of that bowl from the bathroom cupboard? It's one I like to use for shaving.'

Douglass face was glowing, but he didn't say anything.

'And you wouldn't by any chance have seen a little rug that's usually in the box by the front door? It's strange, it's completely vanished.'

Douglas remained still this time, but his face was on fire. As much as he wanted to, he couldn't look away from his dad. He had been so excited about coming home. Now it felt as though the floor had fallen in.

'I happened to be down at the shed after lunch, Douglas – I was looking for something else. I found all those things, and the goose.'

It would have been impossible for Douglas's face to go any redder.

'You should have asked me, son.' His dad didn't shout; instead, his voice was quiet, and somehow that was even worse. 'You should have asked me before taking what's not yours. Imagine if I went to your room and took things without asking. How would you feel?'

Douglas blinked. He had never thought of it like that.

'I didn't know what to tell you about the goose,' he said softly.

John nodded. He shrugged his shoulders and nodded again. Then neither of them said anything for a bit, and Douglas heard his heart thudding under his jumper. Everything was so strange. Thoughts of what he should say flitted into his mind and left again. It was like he was back in school, writing a sentence and then rubbing it all out again.

Nothing seemed right or good enough.

'I'm sorry,' he mumbled at last, looking up at his dad.

*

It was almost nine o'clock and time for Douglas to go to bed. He'd kept himself busy with school work after his dad had spoken to him earlier. Trying very hard to stay out of his dad's way, he'd decided to tidy up his room. He normally never tidied up.

A knock on the door pulled Douglas out of his thoughts.

'Put on your jacket and come out with me a minute,' his dad said.

Douglas followed his dad downstairs and put on his shoes and jacket. His dad waited, holding the back door open. Where were they going?

Outside, he saw the garage light was on and the car was parked in the drive. Were they really going somewhere so late? He followed his dad to the back of the garage to a shelf about the height of Douglas's shoulder. It had been a place for dumping old cases and boxes. Now it was all cleared up and empty.

'I thought this would be a better place for your goose. It's warmer here, for one thing. And safer. There are so many broken things and rubbish in that shed. I'll leave the car in the drive; it'll be all right. So, what d'you think? I'll help you up with the basket if you think it's a good idea.'

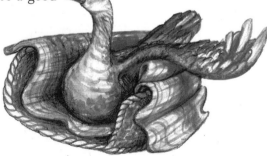

Douglas looked round. It *was* much warmer, and somehow nicer too. And it was easier to get to. He looked at his dad and nodded. Together they went down the garden, past the shadows of the apple trees. In the end, it was easier for John to carry the basket with the goose. Douglas followed behind with everything else. His dad slid the box onto the shelf at the back of the garage. The goose staggered over onto its good side again. Everything was very mucky in the basket.

'I'm afraid geese aren't all that clean,' said John. Douglas could somehow hear his dad smiling even though he couldn't see his face properly as he was looking for something on the higher shelves.

'You do know the goose might not make it?' he whispered as he turned to Douglas. 'But we'll do our best all the same.'

Douglas thought of his mum but remained silent.

'It's funny, seeing that old basket. It makes me think of Teddy the dog. He was my first pet. Have you thought of a name for the goose, by the way?'

'I'm not sure, I'm still thinking. I want to find the right one.'

His dad nodded. 'All right, one thing's for certain – we have to clean that basket. I'll lift the goose and get pecked if you slide the paper underneath.'

*

The next morning Douglas's dad went out to have a look at the goose. He changed the newspaper underneath the bird and got pecked again. The goose was still lying on its side.

After a few minutes, he went back inside and phoned the local veterinary practice to ask if they would come round. In about half an hour, Mark, the vet, carrying a bag, came to the back door, and John led the way round. The two of them talked as they went. They were good friends.

Mark said nothing for some time. He leant over the basket and turned the goose over gently.

'The wing's not broken, but it's obviously damaged. The bird's strong all right, it's not suffering. I can't say for sure what'll happen, John, but there's no harm in trying. It's a boy, by the way! And if the goose already means a lot to your son…'

Meanwhile, Douglas, at school, knew nothing of the vet's visit. He was busy working at sums – the thing he hated most. In between classes, he daydreamed, staring out of the window watching as the wind played and chased; the last russet and golden leaves danced from the trees.

And as Mark the vet left the house and the goose, Douglas was starting an art lesson. They were given charcoal and paper and told they could draw whatever they wanted. The teacher told the class he wanted nature to inspire them. Douglas drew a skein of geese. He had watched them so often coming in over the fields, one goose leading at the head of the V-shaped group. He had watched their heads and wings and feet, learning exactly what they looked like. As his fingers glided over the paper, he thought about his goose and wondered if it had been a leader.

This was when he felt happiest. While drawing, he could forget about everything else, even missing his mum. He didn't find art difficult. It was as if the picture was there already, waiting to appear on the page. He finished in time for the bell to ring, signalling the end of the lesson.

*

'Shall we go visit your mum today?'

It was still half-dark in Douglas's bedroom, early on a Sunday afternoon. Douglas had been napping; he sat up now and rested on one arm.

'Could I take Silverwing with me?' he asked, his voice still sleepy.

His dad smiled. 'So that's the name for your goose? Yes, of course you can – you can hold the basket on your knee.'

As usual, they drove by the back roads. There was a chance they might see a rare bird or an animal, and that day they both saw a bird with bright blue on its wings flying across the road.

'That was a jay!' Douglas's dad said, slowing down. 'We would never have seen it if we had come on the motorway.'

There was no-one else at the graveyard as they pushed open the small wooden gate. The place was unkept: some of the stones leaned to one side, looking as though they might fall.

There were fields on every side, so the graveyard never felt closed in and dark. It was almost part of nature. No-one else in his family was buried here, but this was where his mum had said she wanted to be.

Today it was gusty; the wind seemed to come from so many different directions, strong as a horse. It was hard to walk straight. Douglas battled the wind up the path, struggling a little but carefully carrying the basket with Silverwing in it.

'Why don't you sit for a bit on your own?' his dad suggested. 'I'll not be far away if you want me. I'll be back in a few minutes.'

Douglas nodded. He set the basket down and crouched beside the gravestone. His mum's name was there – Anne – but what he often wished was that it just said Mum. He looked up to make sure his dad was far enough away before whispering, 'This is Silverwing, Mum. I found him, not far from the house.' He looked down at his scarred his hands and smiled. 'I'm still learning how to carry a goose. It isn't easy; he keeps nipping me!'

'What happened to Silverwing?' he thought he heard his mother ask.

'I'm not exactly sure how it happened, but there's something wrong with one of his wings and I want him to get better.' He wanted to say that another way. 'I'll do everything I can to make him fly again, and I'll try to pray, Mum.' He thought about how he'd prayed his mum would get better and that she hadn't, no matter how often and how hard he had pleaded. 'I drew geese in class the other day. I think you'd like the picture.' He didn't know what more to say and his dad was on his way back. 'I wish you were still here, and we could hug like always. I miss you so much, Mum.'

*

When they got back to the house, they found the house shrouded in darkness. The wind must have blown down a power line somewhere, and now the entire village lay in shadow. Douglas fizzed with excitement; he imagined this is what it must have looked like in the old days before electricity reached everywhere.

'Put the goose – Silverwing – back in the garage, and bring in another bucket of coal, Douglas. We'll put the fire on in the sitting room. How about that?'

When Douglas came in with the extra coal, he could hear the fire cracking and spitting. His dad had brought out an old kettle and a tray of shortbread.

'I forgot we couldn't make any tea,' he said. 'We'll boil the kettle over the fire like real campers!'

The fire was burning merrily and the room was warm, like a dragon's lair. John gazed at the dancing flames and thought back to the graveyard visit. He suddenly remembered the chest upstairs. 'Come on Douglas, I want to show you something of your mum's that's in your room, I think.'

The two of them went upstairs with a torch, into Douglas's room, and over to the old chest by the window. It was made of dark wood with metal handles on the sides and nailed dark metal corners on the lid and the base of the chest. There was one keyhole at the front, although the chest wasn't locked. Douglas had never thought about what was inside, and now, as his dad lifted the lid gently, he could see there were folders and folders of old pictures. He knelt beside his dad.

'I couldn't bear to look at these before,' John said softly. 'But your goose has made me remember there's something here you will want to have.'

He rummaged around until he found a box at the bottom. 'This is the one,' he said. 'Come down with me and have a look.'

Back downstairs, they sat in the firelight and flicked through photos of a young girl, not much older than Douglas was now. Could that really be his mum? And there beside her was a goose – a greylag goose just like his.

'Your mum rescued this goose,' his dad told him. 'She loved geese just as much as you do, and she rescued this bird when it was shot and hurt. I'm not sure if it ever flew again or what happened to it.'

John didn't look at him when he spoke and his voice was strange, as if saying some of the words was difficult. Douglas touched his dad's hand to comfort him.

'D'you know if the goose had a name?' he asked shyly.

'Yes,' said his dad, still not looking at him. 'It was called Littlewing.'

3

Even though his dad knew about the goose, Douglas still liked to go out on his own to see Silverwing, especially early in the morning. It was now December, getting colder and colder every day, and when he got out of bed just after half-past seven, it was still completely dark.

Douglas shivered with the cold until he was dressed, then crept downstairs, clicked open the back door and crunched his way on the gravel to the garage.

He had been experimenting with different foods for his goose. He found that Silverwing liked Brussels sprouts better than anything else. His dad gave him leek peelings – they were long and stringy and Silverwing gobbled them up. But potato peelings were not a success at all! Silverwing nosed them about a bit and then simply ignored them.

He liked to talk to the goose as he ate, even though he had to talk above the noise that Silverwing made with his strong beak.

'I hope you have a good day, Silverwing,' he said. 'I wish I could stay and forget all about school, but I can't. When I get back...' but he couldn't quite think what he would do when he came home. 'I wish my mum had known you,' he whispered instead, into the sudden quiet as Silverwing finished his food. His dad called him for breakfast. 'I've got to go now, Silverwing. Hope you feel better. I'll see you this afternoon after school!'

As he rushed into the house, he caught sight of a photograph that his dad had put on the living room mantelpiece. It was of his mother and her goose. The colours had faded from the picture, but Douglas could still feel her warmth every time he picked up the frame. It was as if she was still with him.

*

That night, Douglas's dreams were vivid. He was struggling through a deep forest until at last, he broke out into a clearing. It wasn't dark but it felt like dusk, just before nightfall. When he looked up, he saw his mum; she had come through into the clearing from another side. Her face, her dark eyes and hair were just the same as always, yet there was something different about her.

'Will you come and see Silverwing with me?' he asked, trying to catch hold of her hand. 'Come back home with me, Mum!' He thought she was trying to speak to him, but the words never came. Her hand, though, felt so lovely and warm. 'Do you know why I've called him Silverwing, Mum? Everyone thinks autumn is just one colour, a boring grey, and they think greylags are grey too. But I think they're silvery and magical and ghostly and have so many flecks of different colours and shades. I wish you could stroke Silvering, Mum, he doesn't peck at me now. I'm really gentle with him. You'd like him.' His mum nodded and smiled, slowly slipping her hand out of his, half-turning so he couldn't see her face any longer. In the last second, he saw that she had wings. She flew out of the clearing and was gone.

He woke up drenched in a cold sweat. His special glowing watch on his bedside table said it was five o'clock in the morning. It was still dark outside. He had wanted to tell his mother that they had almost chosen the same names for their geese, but she had gone before he had time.

He recalled waking up on that morning a full year ago, knowing she was no longer there, that she had not gotten better. He had gone up to the wood above the house really believing he would find her, that he would turn a corner and she would be there.

But there was only mist in the trees and the sound of the geese in the distance. Everything was still, otherworldly.

He had an idea as he lay there awake, thinking about his dream. He reached over and switched on the bedside light, got out of bed despite the cold, and stepped over to the old chest with the photographs. Carefully, he took out the photo albums. Right at the bottom was a red book that was smaller and thicker. He'd noticed it when they'd rummaged around for the box of photographs. He picked it out before putting everything else back and closing the lid. Walking back holding the book in one hand, he sat on his bed and pulled the warm duvet over himself. He opened the book carefully. It was a diary.

*

The first page had a little drawing of a goose. It wasn't quite as good as his drawings, but you could just about tell it was a goose if you used your imagination. *'I've decided to call her "Littlewing"'*, his mother had written. *'She's so lovely and soft but she seemed in so much pain from being shot. I'm determined to make her better'.* There were quite a few pages with drawings of the goose and grass, flowers, clouds and hills. One of the drawings seemed to be a little stream with the goose and the sun in the sky with hills in the background. All the drawings had been done with coloured pencils. Occasionally, there was also a drawing of a little cottage.

Towards the end, his mother had written again. *'My father has said that Littlewing won't fly again. I know that may be true, but I don't want to believe it. That means he will never fly back to Iceland for the summer with the other geese. Why do we have to shoot things? Why do we think it is always up to us to decide when wild creatures should live or die? I am still going to try to teach Littlewing to fly again. I have to believe it's possible. I won't say anything to anyone else but they can't stop me hoping and believing.'*

*

That was the end of the book, the left-hand page. Opposite, a feather had been fastened to the paper. Douglas touched it softly with one finger. One of Littlewing's feathers. He thought of what his mum had written and he wondered what had happened, if she had been right or not. He wondered if Littlewing had ever flown again.

It was after the summer last year when he realised she was so very ill. Douglas could see it in her eyes; she still tried to come with him to see things and had to give up halfway. She was tired all the time. He had tried to believe with all his heart that she would get better, but she hadn't. So, it wasn't enough to wish or believe, not always.

He wanted the same for his goose. He wished that it would get better and fly again. But what if it didn't happen? What if his wishes were not enough again and his goose died anyway? He shut the red book, switched off the bedside light and hid in the darkness, but he couldn't escape the fear that whispered in his head.

Douglas sat up again and held his breath. It was getting light outside; it wasn't all that early. He went over to his bedroom window.

Pulling back a corner of the curtain was like opening an advent calendar window. The skies were dark, and falling from them were soft, great flakes of snow.

*

Douglas talked a lot to Silverwing whenever he had the time. He talked to him in exactly the way he had talked to his mother beside her grave. He talked to the goose about school, about the boys who made fun of him in the gym class and about the teacher who shouted because he was no good at football. He told Silverwing about the art class too, about how much he enjoyed drawing and how particularly he liked drawing geese. Not just geese, but the fields and hills and everything else too. That was what Douglas really wanted to do; he was going to be an artist. Then he stopped and thought. Was it going to be enough just to wish for that too? He realised it wasn't. He would have to work hard. Silverwing was scrabbling about for the last leaves of Brussels sprouts in the box. This had to be about hard work too, if he wanted Silverwing to get better and fly again. That was at least a part of it.

One day, Douglas was so lost in thought talking to Silverwing in the dark of the garage that he hadn't noticed that John had come in. Douglas saw he had a lantern in his hand. How much had his dad heard of what he'd said Douglas wondered?

'There's another power cut,' his dad said, walking towards his son, 'and the forecast is for more snow. So, if you're lucky, a day off school tomorrow.' He put his hand on Douglas's shoulder and the two of them turned around. 'It's a bit like Bethlehem,' he said softly. 'I know there wasn't snow in Bethlehem, but it's a bit like the way I imagine it.' He stopped a minute. 'We'll try and have a nice Christmas, Douglas, even though your mum isn't here.' He turned to him. 'What d'you want as a present? What d'you want more than anything else?'

His dad looked at him in the shadows of the garage, and all at once, a wave broke over Douglas. He couldn't see for tears and he cried as if his heart would break. His dad set down the lantern on the garage floor and hugged his son as hard as he could. He held him tight as the waves of wrenching sobs broke over Douglas again and again. Douglas cried for the one present he wanted so desperately and the one present he knew he could never have.

*

'Holly. We're going for holly.'

His dad had come to school to pick him up because there wasn't much time now before it got dark. He saw all the faces of the bullies: George Swinton, Alan Reardon, Tom McCarthy. And there was the worst of the girls – Abigail Edwards. She stuck out her tongue at him as they drove away from school, up towards the wood.

'I have your boots and an old jersey in the back of the car,' John said.

The road was almost clear of snow; what was left was slushy, like marzipan. But there were still lumps in the trees. Douglas was happy to be with his dad and away from school.

They trampled along the woodland path together, as quiet as they could be. That was the best way to see things. Douglas grabbed his dad's elbow and pointed away over to the right. Three deer were standing watching them.

They stood stock-still for a few seconds, and then turned and vanished into the trees.

They found the holly trees and began clipping off little bits with red, shiny berries. The holly was sharp, sometimes it pricked their fingers.

'We'll pick a bit more than we need,' said Douglas's dad. 'We can give some to Mr Somerville, and to Mrs Ferguson across the road.'

Douglas nodded. Mr Somerville was afraid of falling in the snow and didn't come out much. Mrs Ferguson was very old and lonely and always enjoyed a visit by Douglas and his dad.

The snow began again before they finished, but now what fell was quite different – it was like tiny ice needles. Douglas turned his face up to the sky and closed his eyes. The flakes fell like soft hair and brushed his cheeks and mouth. He thought there should be lots of words for snow, not just one. There were so many different types of snowflakes. He'd read somewhere that Inuits had almost fifty words for different types of snow! He was still thinking about the best made-up word for this kind of snow when his dad came up behind him.

'Douglas,' he said. 'I have an idea.'

*

The pictures of Douglas's mum and her goose, Littlewing, had been taken about ten miles away, at the top of a hill track. Her dad had been a gamekeeper; he had looked after the estate lands, making sure fences were mended, watching out for poachers, and keeping an eye open for foxes. The family lived in a small cottage high up on the hillside. It was called Applegarth. When Douglas's mum lived there everything had to be done by lamplight after it got dark, there was no electricity. But when she was fifteen her dad had been given a different house much closer to the village; it was more modern, with electricity and a telephone. The old cottage on the hill was left empty. No-one ever went to live there again.

'Here's my idea, Douglas,' his dad said. They had finished supper and were sitting by the fire. The holly they had gathered was in a big cardboard box, ready to be sorted out and shared with their neighbours.

'It would mean quite a lot of work. We'd take everything with us – and Silverwing of course – and we'd go up to Applegarth for Christmas.'

Douglas's eyes lit up. He had seen the place where his mum grew up, but he'd never actually been inside.

'I'll need to check with the estate,' his dad warned him. 'It will be very cold, Douglas, and you'll have to help with getting everything ready for us to stay. But it might be an adventure.'

There was no doubt in Douglas's mind. It was the most exciting thing he could imagine. He said yes about ten times, promised he would help, asked about all sorts of things his dad didn't know the answer to, and then his dad reminded him he had a goose to look after.

'I'll phone the estate while you go and feed Silverwing,' he said.

John was worried he might have built up his son's hopes for nothing. The estate might say no. The place hadn't been lived in for years. Perhaps Applegarth wasn't even safe? He watched Douglas go out the back door singing, and all he could do was hope. He'd phone the new gamekeeper.

Outside, Douglas had told Silverwing the whole story, totally forgetting to whisper. When he came back inside, he didn't say anything, just looked at his dad.

'We can go,' John said softly. 'We'll head out there on Christmas Eve.'

4

It was the last day of school. There was a Christmas tree in the hall, lit up and covered with tinsel, a star glittering at the top. At eleven o'clock in the morning, they all came in to sing carols. Douglas could see the snow through the windows and right up to the hills above the village. He thought of his mum, of how she had come to this school too, and he wondered how she had got here every day. There were no big roads then, no mobile phones or modern cars.

'I hope you're all going to have a very special holiday,' said Mrs Anderson, their headteacher. 'I hope you'll have a happy time with your families, and that you'll remember this is a time to be especially kind, not just to the people we like –it's easy to be nice to friends and family – but to other people too. It's harder to be nice to the people who are different, who we may think are strange, but that's what we have to remember. That's the real message of Christmas.'

The final shrill bell of term rang, and although all the teachers were calling out to them to walk quietly and keep in rows, nobody listened. Children were shouting and screaming; they pushed their way out of the gym hall and Douglas felt an elbow in his ribs and someone kicking his heel. He turned round to see who it was and caught sight of Alan Reardon's face, laughing. He and Tom McCarthy were together, but he

couldn't hear what they were saying. They were both trying to kick his feet and trip him up.

He got out to the corridor and started fighting his way towards his coat and bag. A teacher was somewhere close by, shouting instructions to the little ones and clapping her hands. Douglas reached his bag and then looked up, into the face of Abigail Edwards. She had been waiting. She had seen him coming. His hands were shaking.

'Hope you have a nice holiday, Douglas,' she shouted in his face. 'Oh, sorry, forgot your mum won't be there, will she!'

And she and Tom McCarthy and Alan Reardon shrieked with laughter and disappeared together along the corridor, looking around at him as they went.

*

He didn't tell his dad about the red book. He wasn't even sure why – he just didn't. He felt his mum had given the book only to him, a present from her. He kept the book under his bed and he looked at it first thing in the morning and last thing at night. Littlewing and Silverwing. He touched the goose feather on the last page of the book and wondered what had happened. She believed her goose would fly again, even though she had been told there was no hope.

On Christmas Eve, he felt so excited. After lunch they packed box after box – holly and lanterns and torches and food. He had to pack a rucksack with all his cosiest jumpers. The boxes piled up in the hall.

'Now, if Santa could only deliver all of that straight to the cottage,' his dad said, clapping him on the shoulder and smiling ruefully.

'I think the reindeer have enough to do,' Douglas said.

Together the two of them packed the car. Douglas would carry Silverwing on his lap. They were almost ready, and it was just beginning to get dark.

'Matches!' his dad remembered and rushed off to find them. That would have been a disaster: no fire, no dinner, no bedside lamps.

They drove up out of the village. The car felt weighed down. It wasn't late but everything felt hushed, everyone was waiting for Christmas. They drove past the last house and Douglas looked back into the valley. There was no other car on the road. It was like it might have been a hundred years before. They turned off onto a single-track road and the car whined and bumped its way along, hedgerows on either side lit and then unlit by the car's headlights in an unsteady pattern.

There were a lot of potholes and twists and turns so his dad drove the car slowly and carefully. Douglas jumped out and opened the large iron gate that creaked a little as he swung it wide. They crossed a river whose banks were thick with snow.

At last they reached their destination. Douglas could just make out the outline of the white cottage. John switched off the engine. It was half-past seven but the darkness outside meant it felt much, much later. He switched on his torch and they got out and started taking all the stuff to the door. Other than their soft steps sinking in the snow, there was complete silence.

*

It was good snoozing by the light of the real fire. The logs were still glowing gently in the grate. They looked like dragon eyes.

It had taken a whole hour to get everything in and sorted. It was so much harder doing everything by candlelight. Douglas kept on forgetting and going to switch on a light. They sorted the kitchen first, then the little bedrooms at the top of the steep stairs.

'This was your mum's room,' his dad said quietly. 'You can have it, Douglas. There's no curtain for the window, I hope you don't mind?'

Douglas shook his head. He liked that. He could lie on the bed later and could look right down over the valley.

At the back of the house, there was a small porch. He reckoned this would be the best place for Silverwing and, using the glove, he fed his goose a good meal. He was getting better at this now and seldom got his fingers nipped. Silverwing still seemed weak on one side, but not as much as when Douglas first found him. That seemed a long time ago now – ages and ages.

He said goodnight to his goose and helped John with the fires. He yawned, hoping his dad wouldn't notice. He was tired but he didn't want to sleep. This was too exciting. John heated some milk over the fire in the living room and they sat hunched close to the flames, sipping piping hot cocoa.

Douglas mulled over a question as they sat in silence.

'Are you glad we came here, Dad?' he asked shyly.

John looked at him and nodded. 'I'd never have thought of it if it hadn't been for your goose and looking at the old pictures in your mum's old chest. It's all thanks to your goose. Yes, I'm very glad. I think your mum would be happy too. Perhaps she knows.'

*

Even though Douglas hadn't wanted to sleep right away, it was exciting having a real fire even in his bedroom. His little pocket torch lay on the bedside table, just in case! He had cuddled into the blankets on the bed, looking at the red glow of the fire, and a moment later he was asleep.

Across the hall in the other small room, John fell fast asleep too. But about three in the morning he lay half-awake, aware of strange shadows. He was lying on his back, the curtainless window ahead of him. He noticed a strange light in the sky, so he got up and walked towards the window.

The room was freezing now the fire had gone out. He stood beside the window, shivering. For a few minutes, he watched the skies amazed, and then he knew he had to wake Douglas. He scrambled into warm clothes then headed to the other bedroom.

'You have to come and see this!' he whispered, shaking Douglas gently.

Douglas sat up, still groggy from sleep. At first, he had no idea where he was. Whimpering from the cold, he pulled his clothes and shuffled moodily downstairs behind his dad. He grumbled under his breath, angry at being woken up. He had been so cosy – why were they going out in the middle of the freezing night? He staggered outside into the snow, his feet scrunching on the layer of frost. His dad stood behind him and put his arms around his shoulders, holding him close, and bent his head to whisper in his ear.

'Look up above the trees – no, further to this side. Right up, there – follow my finger. That's the north. D'you see the light? Coming and going, rising and falling? There, there was another! A green-blue colour – very, very faint. Now I know you think waking you was the worst thing in the world, but I wanted you to see the Northern Lights. Look – that one was dark red!'

Douglas stopped grumbling and looked up. He could see them; shadows rising up and down like ghosts. They were beautiful and strange, like nothing he had ever seen before. It was a silent dance with waves of different colours coming and going, swaying and snaking their way across the night sky.

They watched for half an hour until it got too cold, then they went back up into the darkness of the house and Douglas buried himself in his blankets.

*

Usually, when he woke up, Douglas's first thought was Silverwing. But that Christmas morning it was the crinkling at the bottom of his bed. His second thought was just how cold it was in the room, but his first thought was definitely the crinkling. He had to deal with the second thought before the first, so he got up and tried to scrabble about to find a jumper. He kept on wanting to switch on a bedside light that wasn't there. It was still dark outside so the room was strange and shadowy. After a useless few minutes of rummaging without seeing anything clearly, he lit the candle his dad had given him. He took great care when striking the match, and though the candle wasn't the same as a light bulb, it did help. He cosied up in bed again, a thick woollen jumper over his thin pyjama top. Now he could work out what the crinkling had been.

He thought he knew what it might be – a stocking with all sorts of little presents. The year before there hadn't been one; but he hadn't noticed, it had all been too soon after his mum's death. His dad had given him a small present – he hadn't forgotten him – but neither of them had felt Christmas could be the same. There had been no snow, just rain and gales, so it hadn't even felt like winter in the end.

Douglas remembered going out in the middle of the night to see the Northern Lights! It felt like a dream now. So, the stocking must have been put there after they came in; it definitely hadn't been there when he first went to bed.

At the top of the stocking was a little book of puzzles. Next, there was a bag that was difficult to get out. What on earth was inside? At last, he got it out – a bag of Brussels sprouts. That had to be for Silverwing, not him! He smiled. Below that was what felt like another book. He slid it out carefully, bit by bit, and gasped when it appeared. It was a little sketchbook with a leather cover the colour of dark honey. He caught the scent of it as he held it. Douglas thought he knew where he could have found a book like that. A wonderful antique shop in the village where they sold treasures that looked as good as new. Below the book was a little box of charcoal. And finally, in the toe of the large stocking, was a fat, juicy tangerine.

*

Douglas first thought of waking his dad right away to tell him about his stocking. He went across the passage and opened the door of the other bedroom. He was about to open his mouth when he realised his dad was fast asleep. He didn't have to wake him now. He tiptoed out again and closed the door without a sound.

He returned to his room and he saw all the gifts from the stocking strewn over the makeshift bed. He looked again at the really big present, the drawing book and the box of charcoal. He saw the bag of sprouts too. The cogs in his brain started turning. He put on his warm gloves and slippers.

He took the three gifts and went downstairs. He could see his breath in the cold. He went through to the little porch at the back of the house, expecting to find his goose wide awake and waiting for breakfast. But instead, Silverwing was lying on one side, the good side, his beak tucked into his wing. He was fast asleep. It was still shadowy in the back porch, but there were more windows so it was easier to see. Douglas's heart thudded behind the thick jumper. His idea was going to work after all.

There was an ancient wicker chair in the back porch. Douglas sat down on it and got ready. His hands were really freezing now as he'd had to take his gloves off for this. He cupped them and breathed warmth into them. Then he began to draw. He wanted to capture Silverwing like that before the goose woke up, and he knew he had to work quickly. His fingers were trembling. Time seemed to stand still, just as it did in the art class. He captured the shadows under Silverwing's beak where it tucked into the feathers of the wing. He found Teddy's old basket the hardest bit; twice he got it wrong and had to start again. He had to make it as accurate as he could; his goose really had to look nestled there.

When it was done, he kept looking at it; his heart beat hard now because he was excited. He crept upstairs to his dad's room. John was just turning over, beginning to wake.

'Happy Christmas, Dad,' he murmured, and he knelt beside him to give him the drawing.

5

'All right, it's a beautiful day – you and I are going on another adventure!'

The living room fire was burning fiercely; Douglas couldn't see his breath anymore. Silverwing had had half the bag of sprouts and they had eaten a special breakfast – shortbread and cocoa, and an orange each.

'What are we doing then?' he asked, curious.

'Surprise.'

That was all his dad would say.

'It has to do with your present, I mean your main present. That's still hidden in the car. Go and get ready and I'll see you out there in ten. Wrap up warm.'

Douglas changed the paper under his goose and gave Silverwing one more sprout. Then he put on all the warmest clothes he could find, even a bright red woollen hat his Auntie Elsie had once given him.

'You look a bit like a holly berry,' his dad said when he got into the car.

But it didn't matter. There was no Alan Reardon or Abigail Edwards to see him now. The car started up the track. Douglas realised that the track went much higher even than where the cottage was. They went on, through the opening with birch trees on either side, snaking up the hill. The car didn't like the track very much; it skidded in the muddy snow and Douglas's dad drove very slowly and carefully. Douglas had to keep wiping the windscreen because it got so fogged up. Then, all of a sudden, a bright red sun burst over the top of the faraway hills and everything in its path was made rosy. John had to shield his eyes. They came to a river and he slowed the car.

'I think this is as far as we should go,' he said. 'We can walk the rest of the way. Come on, I'm dying to show you your present!'

They got out. The only sound was the chatter of water over stones.

His dad took a big package out of the boot of the car. It wasn't a very neat parcel but that didn't matter. Douglas bent down to unwrap it with his gloved hands, but that wasn't going to work. With his bare hands, he ripped off the paper. Douglas gasped. It was a wooden sledge!

'This belonged to your granddad,' John said, crouching down beside him. 'I've mended it, made sure it works, and now it's yours.'

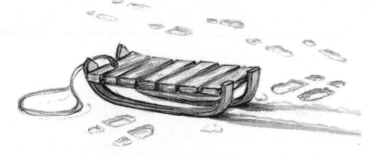

*

By the time they got to the top of the hill and turned around, the car looked as small as a toy. They couldn't see Applegarth at all, but a thin trail of smoke rose into the sky from behind a steep hillside.

'Ready?' his dad asked, once they'd got their breath back. 'I'll get on at the front and you sit behind me. It might be a bit slow the first time.'

But it wasn't. The snow wasn't deep on the hill, and it was crisp after several nights of frost. The sledge picked up speed and Douglas clung on as tightly as he could. His dad yelled something he couldn't make out and all at once they rolled over into a heap and the sledge ran on ahead of them. John couldn't stop laughing, and nor could Douglas, even though they both knew they would have to go the whole way down to bring back the sledge. His dad lay on his back and made a snow angel, sweeping his arms up and down. He was covered in snow from head to foot.

'I'm too old for this,' he said. 'I'll never get up again!'

Douglas gave him a hand, and in the end, they panted their way back up to the top of the hill, dragging the sledge behind them. This time John promised to steer better. They set off and Douglas felt the breeze in his face. They went over a first bump and let out a whoop of joy; now they were steering between pine trees and the red sun flickered through the branches onto their faces. Douglas was elated. It was Christmas Day and he was with his dad. He didn't want this ever to end.

'One more,' he begged when the sledge finally ran out of steam.

'If you peel the potatoes, put crosses in the sprouts, set the table and do all the dishes.' John looked at him with one eye closed which always meant he was only joking, but Douglas still said yes.

On that last run, he thought how much he wished you could slow down time. He wished you could speed it up when things were bad, but now he wanted to slow it down, to make all this last as long as he possibly could. Then he thought of his mum. Douglas wished she could have watched them, that she could have been with them. He missed her so badly it hurt. His dad ruffled his hair and spoke to him with such gentleness.

'Come on. Let's go back and make it a special day, a day to remember.'

*

By four o'clock it was dark. It had been the strangest Christmas dinner either of them had ever had, because all of it had to be cooked or heated over open fires. In the end, Douglas's dad had set old pans over two different fires in the house. There was no table, so they had eaten dinner crouched on the floor in front of the living room fire. But the mantelpiece was still there and it had a whole line of candles. When they had finished eating, Douglas asked if they should do the washing up.

'We'll do it in the morning,' his dad said. 'Easier in the light.'

Douglas wasn't sure if that was an excuse, but he didn't argue.

'Can I bring Silverwing through?' he asked, remembering his goose. He knew Silverwing had no idea it was Christmas, but somehow it didn't seem fair leaving him out. John nodded and Douglas carried him through.

'To think some people have goose for Christmas dinner!' his dad said, looking at Silverwing, who was nosing for a piece of sprout in the basket. Then John looked over at his son and his voice was soft and serious.

'Are you going to be able to say goodbye to your goose, Douglas – if he can fly in the end? Are you ready for that?'

'I want Silverwing to be happy. I found him with an injured wing and I want to make him better. It's just the same as it was with Mum and Littlewing. She wanted her goose to get better, that was the only thing that really mattered.' He didn't know what else to say and he kept watching Silverwing.

His dad nodded. He rocked on his heels where he sat and nodded.

'In a way, it must have been much harder for your mum. Her dad was a gamekeeper and he used to shoot geese. Your mum hated anything to be shot – she had a soft heart just like you. So maybe it was even harder for her to keep the goose to begin with.'

Douglas nodded. He thought of the red notebook and the goose feather.

'It was a hard life in those days,' his dad went on. 'There wasn't much money at all. People who lived on the land were tough with animals – not cruel, but tough. They had to survive. Keeping a pet goose would have been a very, very unusual thing. Especially here in that family.'

Douglas thought about all that for a bit. He stared into the orange flames and he still could hear his goose nosing about in the basket. He thought about his mum's dad, Grandpa Jim, who he'd never met. He had died just before Douglas was born. He could just remember his other grandpa, Grandpa Tom, his dad's dad. He had been kind and full of games and laughter. It was that grandpa who had made the sledge.

'What was Mum's dad like?' he asked in the end. His face burned from the heat of the fire, so he moved away a little.

John sighed and thought for a long time, working out what to say.

'It's difficult to answer, Douglas. You know how it would be if I asked you what Abigail Whatshername is really like. Because she's horrible to you it would be hard for you to be honest about her. It's not that your grandpa was horrible to me, but he didn't like me for a long time. He made it very hard for me to see your mum in the beginning.'

'Why?' Douglas asked. His dad didn't answer at once but stared hard into the flames.

'I wasn't from the land. My dad, your other grandpa, he worked in a bank. I had grown up in the village. I didn't know about buzzards and rabbits and ferrets; I had never set a trap or shot anything. I think your mum's dad thought real men were able to hunt. I think he wanted your mum to meet someone who would do all of those things – maybe a shepherd or a farmer or even someone like him, a gamekeeper. For a long time, I wasn't even allowed to go to the house. Your mum and I had to meet in secret. And once your grandpa caught me!'

John laughed, his face shone in the firelight.

'What happened?' Douglas asked, shuffling closer to his dad on the floor. 'Please tell me, Dad!'

'All right. I'll make some tea first and then I'll tell you.'

48

*

Once they'd had their tea, Douglas's dad went upstairs with a torch. He came back with a bundle in one hand.

'I brought some of Mum's pictures up from our house,' he said. 'I wanted you to get a sense of what it was like when she lived here.'

He sat down beside Douglas and opened three packages carefully. The photos showed his mum as a little girl. She had long hair and was holding a cat in her arms. The cat looked almost as big as she was.

'That cat was called Bawdruns,' his dad told him. 'It was the first pet she was allowed to have. But he wouldn't have been just a pet. He had to earn his keep by catching mice. And he wouldn't have been allowed to stay in the house. He would have had a place out in the shed and he would have got the odd saucer of milk.'

Douglas then remembered his dad had forgotten what he was going to tell him before. 'But you didn't tell me the story, about grandpa catching you! Please, you promised!'

'Well, your granny and grandpa were supposed to be going to the big town one Saturday. Your mum got a message to me the day before that they'd be gone all day. I turned up at the house and walked right in the front door – I didn't even knock. Your grandpa was so furious he got his gun out of the cupboard and chased me around the house three times! I was scared out of my wits, but I don't think the gun was loaded. He chased me right out of the garden and I didn't see your mum again for nearly a month. I missed her so badly.'

John stared into the fire and Douglas watched him for a moment. He knew his dad was sad; he was thinking about how much he missed her now too. Douglas hadn't really thought about that before. He had only thought about how *he* missed his mum.

'And how did you get grandpa to like you in the end?' Now his dad was smiling again. He turned around with a broad grin on his face before putting a big log on the fire.

'Are you ready for another story then?' he asked.

Douglas smiled. Of course he was ready!

'Your grandpa told your mother I could come to the house again on one condition. I had to come with a fish, a fish I'd caught myself without help from anyone.'

Douglas frowned, thinking. He had never seen his dad with a fishing rod and he couldn't imagine him fishing. It was a very weird thought indeed. His dad knew exactly what he was thinking.

'Nobody in my family fished, Douglas! He was right – we were all townies! It wasn't my fault I couldn't fish – nobody taught me. But I would have done anything to see your mum, so

I borrowed all sorts of books from the library and found out where I could get a fishing rod. Then, I went to the lake in the hills where I had been told there were lots of fish. I was so nervous I tripped and fell and got soaked even before I'd started! I remember it was a miserable day, cold and wet, and all I wanted to do was go home and have a bath. I could hardly move my fingers they were so frozen.'

'But did you get a fish in the end? Was it worth it?'

His dad smiled and shook his head. 'I caught a fish that was the size of your pinkie, Douglas. I think that fish felt sorry for me and decided it would jump onto the end of the line. So that was what I came back with.'

'And what did grandpa say?'

'He roared with laughter. Your granny said he had never laughed so much in all his life. He laughed until he cried. He said he was going to stuff that fish and put it in a tiny glass case, though in the end the cat got it. But it didn't matter. I think in a way he was proud of me for what I'd done. From then on, I was allowed to go to the house and see your mum. It took a long time, but he finally accepted me.'

Douglas nodded. But now his mind was on two things – Littlewing and Silverwing. And his grandpa.

'What do you think he would have thought of me?' Douglas asked.

'I think he would have been proud of you,' his dad said. 'Look what you've done for your goose. Silverwing isn't flying again, but he's a lot stronger than when you first found him. There's still a long way to go, but you've worked hard and did the best you could. You've gone out early in the morning in the dark; you've gone out at night when it was snowing. I really think he'd be proud of you, Douglas, even if he didn't tell you he was. He never really gave compliments; he didn't know how to.'

Douglas listened hard. He looked at his dad waiting for him to continue.

'And I'll tell you another thing he'd be proud of: your drawing. He was good at doing little sketches of wildlife, but he never really had a chance to learn. He left school at fourteen, not much older than you. But you have a real gift and he would be very proud of that. If he were still alive, he'd take you to see eagles and otters and all sorts of animals. And you *have* got talent, Douglas – real talent. That drawing you gave me is amazing. And most of all, your mum would be proud – that's for sure.'

John's voice cracked with emotion as he spoke. Douglas just nodded. What a strange Christmas Day it had been. Like nothing he had ever believed it might be, but it was good – special.

'So, are we going back down to the village tomorrow? Please can we stay one more night, dad?' Douglas begged. 'I love it up here and we might never come back, this might be the only time.'

John nodded. 'We don't have all that much food, but we can graze on leftovers. All right, we'll stay tomorrow night too. Come on, let's get a good, long sleep. I'm still sore after all that sledging!'

When they went upstairs, Douglas sat by the window in the room that had been his mum's. He thought about all the questions he wanted to ask her. He had learned so much, but he wanted to know so much more about her life when she was his age.

*

6

Boxing Day was always depressing for Douglas, but this year it seemed worse than ever. Christmas Day was over, that was no different to other years, but everything now felt completely dull and miserable. The fires that had burned so merrily had turned to ash and every room in Applegarth was freezing. In the kitchen, all the dishes lay piled in a heap, unwashed and stuck together. Outside it was drizzling. But more than anything and everything else that morning, Douglas missed his mum. Her presence was everywhere in the house. It was like so often when he had believed he would see her in the garden of their house, or in the woods, and she'd be there, coming to meet him. Now he felt he should be able to go upstairs and hear her voice, calling him. She was so nearly there and yet she wasn't there at all.

His dad still wasn't up so Douglas he let him sleep. He found his precious new drawing pad and box of charcoal, and he went back to sit in the wicker chair to do another drawing of Silverwing. But his goose was wide awake, moving constantly about the old basket, never in the same position for more than a few seconds, so Douglas gave up in despair. His hands

were red with cold anyway; it was hard to hold the charcoal.
He went back into the living room, thinking he'd give his dad
a surprise by getting the fire lit again, but it was a messy job
and all he managed to do was get his hands and face filthy.
He was cold and miserable and he missed his mum so badly.
He cried there where he sat, crouching by the old hearth. And
that was how his dad found him twenty minutes later. He
crouched down beside his son and reached out for his freezing
cold hands.

'Forget the fire, I'll do that. You worry about that goose of
yours. I reckon he needs a bit of exercise and I want you to try
to take him for a walk. By the time you get back, I'll have had
a think about what we can do today.'

He hugged Douglas tight and ruffled his hair. Douglas
tried to smile. He put on a huge jumper and his boots and his
extra-thick gloves to go outside. His dad went into the kitchen
and came back with a saucer of pieces of Brussels sprouts.

'That's for Silverwing,' he said, 'but just one bit at a time.'

*

Douglas quickly got a hang of the plan. The way to lure
Silverwing into walking a bit further was to crouch with a
bit of sprout a few yards away. Silverwing looked up, saw the
open hand with the tempting bit of veg, and reluctantly began
to waddle over. His goose still wasn't steady on his feet and
still seemed to lean to one side. But his dad was right that
Silverwing was stronger; there was no doubt about that.

A picture flashed into Douglas's mind. He saw his mum
crouching on these same stone steps at the back of the house,
trying to get her goose to walk and become stronger. He felt so

certain that that was how it had been, and he imagined his granddad at the back door, watching. His grandpa had shot geese, and he thought just how hard it must have been for his mum to be allowed to keep an injured goose. Grandpa Jim must have been very stubborn indeed.

As he crouched in the wet snow, trying to lure his goose a little further, he heard the sound he recognised. He looked up into the sky and saw a skein of geese, calling as they flew. They were right above him, just as the geese had been the day they had gone to visit his mum's grave. Silverwing paid them no attention at all and Douglas couldn't help laughing. Sometimes his goose was like a grumpy old man. He held out his hand.

'Come on, Silverwing! It's your favourite! Come on, you can do it!'

His goose lurched over one more time and gobbled up the bit of sprout. Then Silverwing

lay down on his good side and would go no further. Douglas crouched and talked to him in a low voice, saying he had done well and that next time they

would go further. Silverwing tucked his beak into his beautiful wing feathers and sighed. Douglas stopped talking and looked around at the back wall of the house. He could see something glinting. Intrigued, he got up to look.

There was a key lying on the stones, right against the house wall. It was about the length of his pinkie; smaller than a shed key. He turned it over in his hands. Where on earth did it come from?

*

It was much harder to get Silverwing back into the house than it had been to get him out of it. Nothing seemed to work and after a long time of waiting, Douglas gave up and carried his goose back. He got one bad nip – Silverwing was still a wild goose, that was for sure. He put him down gently in Teddy's old basket and left him the last three pieces of sprout on the saucer. He'd kept the key safe in one of his pockets and couldn't wait to show it.

'Look what I've found, Dad!'

John wasn't sure where it came from. He thought it might be from one of the sheds at the back, or that it had just been dropped by someone. It might be that it had nothing at all to do with the house.

In the living room, there was a roaring fire with a sizzling pan of bacon on top. They had two rolls and a piping hot mug of tea each.

'Now, while you were out, I had an idea about what else we could do,' his dad said. 'Your mum once showed me a place where she used to go sliding, and I reckon the ice'll be strong enough. So why don't we do the dishes first and then wrap up and see what it's like? We'll need to walk there.'

The dishes didn't take as long as Douglas had feared. His dad washed and he dried. The house was feeling warmer now and outside there was a tiny bit of blue sky in all the grey.

Maybe it would turn bright after all. They packed a lunch and made a flask of tea and changed into their warmest clothes.

Douglas left the little key beside his bed. It winked silver in the light, just as when he had seen it first, and he wondered again where it had come from. Maybe his dad was right; maybe it wasn't from the house. His dad called him to hurry and he forgot about everything else. He put on his red woollen hat from his Auntie Elsie and they were ready to go.

He told his goose where they were going and Silverwing didn't seem the least bit interested. He just looked at Douglas with one eye and then went back to sleep. He had plenty of food if he was hungry. Douglas said goodbye and closed the door gently.

'I think I remember how to get there. It's up through the wood and over the hill. I remember a red gate. I think we follow the track the whole way.'

*

They arrived at an old skating pond with shallow frozen water. It hadn't been all that easy to find, though. His dad had been right about a red gate, but not right about following the track the whole way. After the red gate, there was a little path that led through the woods. The pond was completely hidden amongst tall birch trees.

Douglas could take a long run and then slide the whole length of the pond. He let out a whoop of delight and a whole flock of pigeons scattered from the trees. He kept sliding until he was out of breath and his face glowed with warmth. Then he went back to his dad and lay on his back until he had his breath back, staring up at the clear blue sky above them.

'Listen,' John whispered.

There was a murmur of breeze in the trees followed by complete stillness. Douglas realised they hadn't seen another person since Christmas Eve. It was amazing when you thought of all the millions of people in the world, and it now seemed like they were the only two souls in existence. Douglas sat up on his elbows and pondered quietly for a bit.

'Did Mum miss living up here, when they moved to the village?' he finally asked.

'I know she did,' John said. 'I remember her telling me. She said she cried for two whole weeks. She used to come back whenever she could, just to see Applegarth and to come to places like this. But in the end, she had to start a new life. It was too sad coming to see an empty house.'

Douglas imagined what it must have been like.

'Can we come up here more often, Dad? I mean to explore, to find places like this that Mum knew? I like it, it feels right.'

John looked at him and he nodded, understanding the feeling.

'Absolutely we can. I feel the same, even though it can be hard at times. We'll come up and explore as often as you want to.' He paused. 'Come on, let's have some lunch and then get back before it's dark!'

*

That evening they had cocoa and a piece of Christmas cake in front of the orange embers of the fire. Douglas made sure his goose was all right and then they both took a lit candle each for their bedside tables, blew the rest out and went upstairs.

They had made fires in the bedrooms and Douglas put a new log onto his fire before he got ready for bed. He was determined to watch the flames once he was tucked up; he wanted to remember their last night here for as long as he could. Tomorrow life would go back to normal.

He managed a few minutes and then he almost drifted off. He shook himself awake but his eyelids were heavy and this time he did fall asleep. He dreamed he was drawing in the art room in school. He was drawing a whole skein of geese on one great big sheet of paper and he knew that all the bullies were watching him. They were laughing at him, calling him all the worst names they could think of, but he didn't turn round – he kept on drawing. He knew in his heart the drawing was for his mother. It was a present for her.

He opened his eyes with a start and wondered what it was that had woken him. He was lying on his back and the moon was shining through the window. The fire had gone out, but the room had turned to silver in the moonlight. He looked at the wall beside him and he saw the light was shining on a keyhole. There was a cupboard in the wall, not quite as tall as he was.

A strange thought went through his mind – what if the key fitted, the key he had found that morning? For a second, he couldn't face the cold; then he made up his mind. He had to know now; he wouldn't sleep again until he did. He flung off the blankets and pulled on his jumper, shivering madly.

He picked up the key and turned it in his hand before placing it in the lock. It fitted! He turned it and the door opened. It was stiff so he had to pull hard and wiggle the key a bit before he could prize it open.

And there on the other side lay a small red notebook.

*

Douglas lit the candle on his bedside. His hands were still shaking. This felt like another dream, but he pinched himself and realised it wasn't. He kept his jumper on and got back into his bed. Then he opened the notebook.

This spring I have been walking with Littlewing every day. My father still says the goose will never fly again, but I can't give up hope – I want Littlewing to be well. I want him to fly back to Iceland with the others. I have to hide away pieces of food for Littlewing; my mother won't give me anything. She says it is a sin to give up food for a goose when there are starving children in the world. She is sometimes stricter than my father. I go out with Littlewing very early every morning, before it's properly light.

Then there was a new date on the handwritten entry, from early February.

In some ways, my father is more interested in the goose than my mother. He still doesn't believe that Littlewing will ever fly again, but now and then he will come to watch the goose at the back door. It's not my father's fault that he shoots so many things; that's what he was taught as a boy. He learned then that there were too many geese and that their numbers had to be kept down. All the other gamekeepers say the same thing, so he's never going to listen to someone like me. But I am almost sure he does see that my goose is intelligent all the same. Perhaps he has learned to look at them in a new way.

This was the next part of the story, the story that had ended in the red book he had found at the bottom of the old trunk at home. But why had the book been left here in the cupboard? He imagined that his mother had known he would come here one day and find it. There were so many things that had happened since he found Silverwing. Had his mother come back to the house after they moved to the village to leave the book and the key here? He might never know.

Littlewing has flown! Just a few yards, but he has flown all the same! My father said nothing when I told him, he just nodded. He normally always has lots to say, but this time I really believe he was lost for words. He was in shock. My mother said nothing when I told her; she still believes Littlewing should never have been kept alive after he was injured. A goose that is shot is for eating, that's what she believes. There is nothing I could ever say to her that would change her mind.

Douglas turned the page, his eyes flickering over the words. He had to read on; he couldn't stop now.

This morning my father came out to see Littlewing. I crept downstairs as usual to see how my goose was, and there was my father. He tried to pretend it was an accident he was there, but I know it wasn't. Littlewing is very restless. The other geese are restless in the fields too; it's almost time for them to fly back to Iceland after the winter. When I walked with him today,

*he was fidgety, looking in every direction. He didn't fly but
he was trying to stretch his wings all the time. My father kept
watching at the back door. Then he disappeared when he saw
my mother.*

Douglas was shivering; it was so cold in his mum's old
room, but he had to know how the story ended. He would
never sleep if he didn't find out! His eyes scanned the words
as quickly as possible, but even in the torchlight it was hard
to read, and his mum's handwriting wasn't always clear. He
forced himself to get up again and put on a second jumper
and a pair of thick socks. He glanced out of the window and
saw everything silver in the moonlight. It was so beautiful. He
thought what it would have been like to grow up here instead
of in the village. Then he thought of how hard his granny and
grandpa had been on his mum. It wouldn't have been easy; in
a way it was a whole different world up here. He imagined
what it would have been like if he'd had to beg his dad to be
allowed to keep Silverwing. But now he was very curious to
know what had happened to Littlewing, his mum's goose.

*This morning I went out a bit later since it was Saturday.
It was a clear day, with a little fresh snow in the hills. My
father was there too, and this time he didn't pretend it was
by accident.*

*I gave Littlewing his food outside, and all at once, we
heard a skein of geese overhead. He lifted his head, tried his
wings, ran as if to get up speed, and then rose into the air.
For the first few seconds, I wasn't sure if he would make it;
I was afraid he might fall, and then he began to beat his
wings. I think I was crying and my father came and put*

his arm around my shoulder. I looked at him and he was nodding, nodding all the time. I was so happy, as happy as I've ever been in my life. Littlewing had flown again after all! He would go back to Iceland with the other geese. It had happened just as I had dared believe it might. I was trying as hard as I could not to cry and the harder I tried the worse it was. It was such a lovely end to the long struggle.

My father did the last thing in the world I expected. He hugged me and he patted my hair. That made me cry all the more. 'There, there, lass,' he said in the end, and his voice sounded odd, unlike anything I'd heard before. Then he said what I never thought he'd say in a hundred years. It was more of a whisper, as if he was afraid someone else might hear him:

'I promise you that as long as I live, I'll never shoot another goose.'

When I turned around, there was Mother, standing in the doorway. She wasn't angry that we hadn't come to breakfast. I think maybe she saw the moment Littlewing flew too. She never said a word about it, but I think that maybe she did. I think both of them look at me a little differently now. It's not that I was right; it's more that I kept on believing.

7

When he went downstairs the following morning, Douglas wanted to believe Silverwing would fly too. His head had been full of his mother's story all night. But his goose didn't even want to come for a walk with him. Silverwing seemed much more content with the warmth of the porch, even after Douglas had sat on the wicker chair and told him in a loud whisper of how Littlewing had flown again. Silverwing was eating the last bit of sprout, and when he was finished, he turned away from Douglas with a sigh and tucked his head in his wing. Douglas knew how hard it was to take a cat for a walk; now he knew it was even harder with a goose.

John listened to the story of the red book and didn't say a word. He let Douglas tell him the whole thing while he looked at the book himself and nodded now and again. When the story was done, he looked up at his son.

'See how your mum kept on believing? She didn't give up hope. We'll take this back home with us and keep the two books together. I think she'd have wanted that. I want to read both of them the whole way through.'

'Why d'you think one of the books was in Mum's old chest and the other one up here at the house? Why weren't they in the same place?'

His dad shook his head and flicked through the pages of the book again. They were a little bit crinkled with age but everything could still be read.

'You remember I told you yesterday that your mum came back to the house? She came back because she missed the place so much.'

Douglas nodded. He saw his mum in his mind's eye; he imagined her up at the old pond and back here at the house, in her old room.

'There was no-one here after they left,' his dad went on. 'Maybe the house was open. Maybe your mum wrote this book in her old room! I don't know, but perhaps she left it here in the end because it was a story that happened here. Somehow it belonged here.'

A noise made them both turn round at the same time. It was Silverwing, he had plodded in from the back porch. They both laughed.

'I think your goose wants a second breakfast! Then we'll need to get packed and go.'

*

When they arrived home the house was as cold as ice. There were one or two messages on the answering machine from people wondering why they weren't at home. Auntie Elsie who had given Douglas the red woollen hat wanted to know if her presents had arrived safely.

It was strange being back home. It was funny switching on electric lights again; Douglas missed being able to light a candle or a lamp. But at least he could still help his dad make a roaring fire in the living room. They put on the tree lights so it felt more like Christmas. It was still the holidays; there were days and days until he had to go back to school.

'Why don't we spread some festive cheer?' John decided. 'We'll go round to the neighbours with a present, just like we usually do before Christmas. The holly's still in the box where we left it!'

That was a good afternoon. Douglas had too much Christmas cake and his dad had too much mulled wine, but there were lots of stories about winter in the old days and snowstorms

and people getting lost, and Douglas was glad they had gone out. He remembered what Mrs Anderson had said about

the real meaning of Christmas, that it was about giving to other people, not just getting presents for yourself.

They went back home and John fell fast asleep in the armchair by the fire. Douglas tiptoed upstairs to find his artist's pad and the box of charcoal.

He sketched his dad with his mouth open and he was pretty pleased with it. He left it on the mantelpiece so his dad would find it when he woke up. Then he remembered his goose; it was time he went out to feed Silverwing.

He put on his boots and switched on the back-door light. Outside, he could hear a light breeze passing over the garden and the field. He'd give Silverwing some sprouts; it was still Christmas after all. He switched on the garage light and quietly went up towards Teddy's old basket. He stopped dead in his tracks. Silverwing wasn't there.

*

Douglas ran inside, banging the door shut behind him. His heart was hammering as he rushed into the sitting room.

'Dad! It's Silverwing!

There's no sign of him! He's gone!' Douglas said, shaking his dad awake.

John jumped up from the armchair, made his way to the back door and grabbed his coat. 'Go and get the big torch, Douglas, the one we had up at your mum's house.'

They went out into the back garden, where the wind hissed through the old apple trees. The torch beam flashed this way and that as John led the way down towards the old shed where Douglas had hidden Silverwing when he first found him. Douglas's hands were sore with the cold. It didn't matter, though – all that mattered was finding his goose. He followed the light of his dad's torch, hoping and hoping he would spy the shape of Silverwing, but there was nothing.

'You don't think someone would steal him, Dad?'

John laughed gently. 'Anyone who tried to steal Silverwing would get one heck of a bad nip! There are easier things to steal than a goose. Perhaps if he was laying golden eggs, but that hasn't happened yet. No, I think we'll find him soon enough.'

After searching every square inch of the garden, they decided to check the old shed. The door had been left open just enough for a goose to squeeze through, and that's exactly what Silverwing had done. Douglas and John were so relieved that they both had to stand and laugh.

'Isn't that typical?' said his dad. 'You do all you can to get an animal – or in this case a bird – as cosy as you can, and it goes back to the very place you took it away from! Come on, we'll try the basket again!'

John carried a very grumpy Silverwing back to the garage and got pecked a good number of times before he got there. But Silverwing seemed to settle in the basket all the same. As they stood there watching, the rain pattered like fingertips on the garage roof. They closed the door this time and went back up to the house. Douglas's heart flooded with relief. He loved his goose. He wondered how he could face watching him fly away.

*

'I think it's a good sign,' John said when they were back by the fireside. Douglas stared at him, open-mouthed. How on earth could Silverwing disappearing be a good thing?

His dad put down his mug of tea. 'Think about it,' he said. 'Your goose was injured; his wing was torn and he must have been in a lot of pain. That was why he was all lopsided. The fact that he's able to get from one place to another, and quite fast, means he's much stronger. Taking him for walks up at Applegarth had a good effect!'

Douglas nodded. It was true; his goose was stronger. He thought again about Silverwing flying away. That was what his mum had wanted for Littlewing, and that's what happened. She had cried, not from sadness, but because no-one had believed except her that her goose would fly again. She had been right after all. Things were different for him. His goose was getting stronger all the time and might well be able to fly, but was that really what he wanted? Of course he wanted Silverwing to be well, but if his goose flew back with the others to Iceland, that would be the last Douglas would ever see of him. For the first time, he thought about how much he would miss his goose. He had done so much for Silverwing since he found him. Douglas had hoped against hope the bird would survive and fly, but now he didn't want to see him go.

He didn't say a word to his dad, but he went to bed that night with all those thoughts circling in his head. He didn't sleep for a long time; tossing and turning in the darkness. He knew what was right but he couldn't help being frightened of losing his goose.

John had noticed Douglas had gone to bed worried, but he hadn't said anything. He wondered if it was coming back home from Applegarth. He wondered if Douglas was missing his mum. What else was bothering him? When he looked in on him at midnight his son was fast asleep, but the blankets were all twisted and muddled. John guessed it was Silverwing. He had a pretty good idea what might be troubling Douglas, but he needed to be sure.

*

In the end, it wasn't difficult to figure out what was wrong with Douglas. In the days before the new year arrived, he didn't go out much with his goose. He made excuses about hail and rain, or he said he wasn't feeling so good, and he spent a lot of time on his own in his room. He said he was drawing, but when his dad said he should come down and draw in the warmth by the fire, Douglas muttered an excuse.

One night, John went upstairs and sat at the bottom of Douglas's bed. He looked at his son tenderly and in a certain way, the way he always did when he wanted to have an honest answer and wouldn't go away without one. Douglas knew that look very well indeed.

'What is it?' John asked. Just those three words, and the look.

Douglas sighed. He turned round in bed but he knew it was useless. He knew his dad would stay until five in the morning if he had to.

'It's Silverwing,' he said, his voice low, muffled by a blanket.

Now his dad came and sat beside him. His voice was different this time.

'I guessed it was Silverwing, but what exactly?'

Douglas sighed again and couldn't look at his dad. He was so confused.

'I want him to fly but I don't. If he flies, then he won't come back.'

And then his eyes filled with tears and his dad hugged him as he cried. When Douglas had run out of tears, John went downstairs and made them both mugs of cocoa. He put on the bedside light and Douglas sat up against his pillow, his eyes red. Still, his dad said nothing. Douglas kept waiting for him to speak.

'I thought you would be angry,' he said. 'That it was bad to think like that.'

'What can I say?' John said. 'I understand completely. I bet I'd feel the same. You want two things and you can't have both. I bet your mum felt the same way. When you love someone, it's hard to let them go. It was the same with your mum. I loved her and I had to let her go; I had to say goodbye, even though I never wanted to. I didn't want her to suffer, but I didn't want to say goodbye either. I could never be angry with you.'

*

Now his dad went with him when they walked Silverwing in the field. Sometimes the walks were frustrating. Silverwing would sit down in the grass and look at them both as much as to say,

'You can try to make me go further, but you're not going to manage!'

And it didn't matter if they tried to lure Silverwing with pieces of sprout, or cabbage or carrot – the goose closed his eyes and ignored them.

'Come on, we'll go for a walk ourselves!' John said to his son.

They walked down to the bottom of the stream in the field and back, their hands deep in their pockets because it was freezing.

On New Year's Eve, the last night of the year, it snowed until the little shed at the bottom of the garden looked like an igloo. Douglas sat at the upstairs window, hoping it would go on and on so there would be no school the following week. But by then the snowploughs had got to work and the blocked roads were cleared.

Douglas sat in the school hall on that first morning, a dark knot sitting in his stomach. The whole term stretched ahead of him.

When he turned around, he caught sight of George Swinton and Alan Reardon. Last of all, he spied Abigail Edwards; she glared at him and stuck out her tongue. He remembered what she had said on that last day before the holidays and it still bothered him. He thought about all the days up at his mum's old house and the days at home. They had seemed to stretch forever, and now they were over.

Mrs Anderson got up and clapped her hands. Slowly, a ripple passed through the classes until not a sound could be heard.

'Welcome back, all of you. I hope you've had a wonderful holiday. The hard work begins again today. I want to remind you about the art competition for all the primary schools in the county. Entries have to be handed in by the end of the week and as  we've lots of budding artists, I want to see plenty of entries! Have a good day in class and remember there'll be no outdoor playtime today because of the snow.'

Douglas got up, his head spinning. An art competition: would he have time to draw a completely new picture? He'd never entered a competition before. His art would need to be really special. His heart hammered in his chest as he went out into the corridor.

*

'I'll tell you what you're going to draw, you're going to draw that goose of yours!' and his dad pointed at Silverwing as they stood together in the garage. 'And your drawing's going to be as good as the one you did for me!'

After school that Monday afternoon, Douglas sat in an old chair in the garage a little way away from his goose. Silverwing wasn't the least bit interested and had his beak tucked into his wing, sighing occasionally. Douglas sat on a blanket and he had another wrapped around his shoulders. He had his Auntie Elsie's red woollen hat on his head. His dad asked if he could take a picture of him, and Douglas said that if he did, he wouldn't dry another dish for the next ten years. John didn't risk it. Instead, he brought Douglas his sketchbook and box of charcoal.

Douglas didn't know where to start. His hand trembled with nerves. He had to forget about the competition. This was just another drawing. It was no different from being in the art room. He had to forget about everything else and find the goose that was hiding in the paper. Twice he began and twice he started again; he had to crumple up the bits of paper and put them under his chair so he couldn't see them. It was going to be dark soon. He had to get it done.

Then it was as if the piece of charcoal began to move in his hand without him trying. First, he sketched out the full outline, his hand a blur over the page. He could start to see his goose peering at him from the page. The angle was different, but it was very like when they had been up at Applegarth, his mum's house, and he had sat on the old wicker chair to draw his goose in the back porch. He then started to fill in the details, starting with the head and working all the way down to Silverwing's webbed feet.

In half an hour he was finished. His hand was trembling again, but it was because he had done it – he had managed it after all. He took the blankets and went back inside. He climbed the stairs slowly, looking at the drawing in his hand as he went. He knew there was nothing he could do to make it any better. He met his dad on the landing and he didn't say anything either, neither of them did.

John looked at the drawing and he looked at his son, smiling.

Douglas beamed with pride. His dad was happy and he had finished his drawing in time for the competition.

8

Once the drawing had been handed in, Douglas's heart felt heavy. Every day he dreaded the taunting of Abigail Edwards and the others; there was nothing he could do to make them leave him in peace. It was as if the Christmas holiday had been a dream that faded. His dad was busy with work and there wasn't time for walks. He looked after his goose every morning and every evening, but at the back of his mind was always the fear that when spring came, Silverwing would fly once more and be gone forever.

Douglas missed autumn when he and his mum used to go for long walks together, before she fell ill and was in and out of hospital. They loved exploring the wood together, looking for conkers under the best of the chestnut trees, and watching for red deer and squirrels and owls.

The wood was another world; it was somewhere the bullies could be forgotten. The silver he loved so much had been washed away by the winter.

Christmas and New Year were over; but there still wasn't a single sign of life in the fields. Spring had yet to arrive.

*

One morning, when Douglas was at school, John called Mark the vet and asked if he would look at the goose again. At lunchtime, the two men went down the gravel drive to the garage as they had before.

'This is a much stronger goose,' Mark said. He sounded surprised.

'Will he fly again?' Douglas's dad asked quietly. 'Is it likely?'

'John, I can't tell you that – I don't know. But there's very little wrong with this goose now – that much I can tell you. Douglas has done well.'

John nodded. Douglas *had* done well. But he was afraid of his son having to lose his goose too. He had lost too much in his life, too much of what he loved. He didn't tell Douglas the vet had visited; there was no reason to upset his son. The goose had brought so much happiness, surely it couldn't all end now?

Outside, the days were still unbearably short and rainy. John had to keep hoping and not give up, but it was hard. He read the little red book Douglas had found in Anne's old room at night to find comfort, and because he hoped he might just find another answer to his worries about Douglas.

Spring came, bit by bit. The streams rushed and chattered with melted snow, and the first ray of weak yellow sunlight shone through the valley. The birds sang again, and even the high hills were clear of snow once more. The days were lengthening at last and the colours that seemed to have gone forever crept back slowly.

In school, Douglas read the Greek myth of Persephone, who was kept prisoner by Hades in the underworld for the winter and then allowed to return to the earth. Her mother, Demeter was so happy to see her once more that she sang for joy and everything came back to life.

Douglas thought of his mother, and of how everything felt like winter still because she wasn't around anymore.

*

In the fields the geese were restless. They flew in their wide skeins each morning and evening as if they were practising, getting their wings ready for the long flight north to Iceland. John watched them and listened to them, but he didn't say anything about them to his son. He didn't know what to say and he didn't know what he hoped for either. He wanted to be a good dad – to make Douglas happy, but there were some things even he couldn't do. He felt that somehow he had failed, but he wasn't quite sure how.

On a beautiful, sunny spring morning John went out to the garage and stood beside Silverwing, who, as usual, was asleep in Teddy's old basket. He stood and watched the goose for a long time. Then he opened the back window in the garage, the little window with its ledge just behind the shelf where Silverwing sat.

Douglas still talked to his goose. In the evening before he began his homework he went and talked to Silverwing about the bullies in school and about being afraid. He spoke as Silverwing snuffled about in the basket for lost bits of food. Sometimes his dad heard him, though he never came close to listen to what he was saying. But he heard the soft murmur of Douglas's voice in the shadows as he stood on the gravel in the drive.

*

It was the afternoon of the school assembly. The hall was loud with children talking and shouting because Mrs Anderson hadn't arrived yet. Douglas's ears hurt with the noise; he wanted it to be over so he could get to art class. He felt his pencil in his pocket and imagined himself drawing all afternoon.

'Hey, wakey wakey, Johnson!'

He was tugged from his daydream by the shrieking of Alan Reardon behind him. The other boys roared with laughter and Alan tried to grab his arm. Douglas shrank away to the end of the bench.

Mrs Anderson came in at last, clapping her hands as she walked, and everyone quietened down at once. Douglas's heart slowed; at least it would be better now she was here. At least the bullies couldn't get him.

'Now, those of you who're involved with swimming practice can leave at half-past – just slip quietly out. But sadly, I have to begin by mentioning the window that was broken at some point over the weekend – I want the culprit to own up before the week is up. I'm afraid it was someone from the school, so please have the courage and the honesty to come to my office and tell me.

'Now, a big well done to all of you who were involved with the chess championship. But the main reason for calling today's assembly is because I have just heard the results of the art competition. One or two of you will be hearing about your runners-up prizes, but I want you to know that the overall winner is Douglas Johnson. He'll be awarded his prize later on in the year, but I want to congratulate him today! This is a huge honour for him and the whole school!'

Clapping erupted around him. A teacher was pushing Douglas to his feet; he was to go out to the front. His head was swimming; everything was strange and far away. And then he saw the face of Abigail Edwards; full of astonishment, complete amazement. He saw the faces of all the bullies as he passed and went to the front, as the whole hall clapped and he shook Mrs Anderson's hand. Everything moved in slow motion; the only thing he could hear was the sound of his heart.

*

Douglas ran all the way home. The bullies watched him but said nothing as he flew past. He was different now; he had won the competition. He couldn't wait to reach home. He thought his heart would burst as he charged into the drive, his feet loud and careless on the gravel. His face was on fire and he was gasping for breath. He stopped for a second then tore on down the drive, towards the garage and the ledge, the basket and his goose – Silverwing. He wanted his goose to know, to know he had done it after all!

'Douglas! Douglas!'

He didn't hear his dad at first. He ran into the dim garage and stood there, dragging the air into his lungs as he searched for Silverwing.

'Douglas, he's gone! Silverwing's gone!'

He didn't understand. He turned and looked at his dad. Gone? How could his goose be gone?

His dad stood beside him and placed his hand on his shoulder.

'Your goose has flown! He's gone back; he's on his way to Iceland!'

Douglas looked at him in disbelief. He turned away, unable to believe his dad's words. Not now, surely 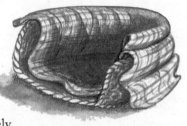 not now? His eyes blurred with tears and he broke away from his dad's hold. He heard him calling his name behind him, begging him to come back, but he couldn't. He had wanted his goose to know. He dropped his bag on the gravel and he went out onto the road, turned and saw the shadow of the wood. That was the only place he wanted to go. The wood where he'd always dreamed he'd see his mother, where he'd find her at last.

He couldn't hear John behind him now. He could only hear his own feet and the thud of his heart in his chest. It was raining and it would be dark soon, but he didn't care – it didn't matter. Silverwing was gone and he didn't get to say goodbye.

This was where he had dreamed he would find her, in the heart of the wood. He remembered his dream, when she was there with him and he talked to her, and when he saw her wings she had gone – flown away, just like Silverwing.

Douglas stood in the half-darkness, hearing the drops of rain pattering against the leaves, and he knew he would never find her there. He had to face up to the fact that his dream was no more than fantasy. He doubled over and cried with grief.

'Dou-glas!'

He heard his dad calling his name a long way off. He didn't want to answer; he didn't want to explain any more. But Douglas knew his dad was worried; he could hear the anxiety in his voice as he called again and again.

In the end, he called back; he opened his dry mouth and answered.

When John found him, he hugged him for a long time. Douglas realised his dad was crying too; his shoulders were shaking. When he let him go Douglas saw that his face was shining, and he knew it wasn't from the rain.

'Why are you crying, Dad?' he asked. He remembered that the last time he had seen him crying had been at the hospital, the night his mum lay dying and there was nothing more they could do for her.

But now John smiled through his tears.

'I'm crying because I love you,' he said. 'I'm crying because I'm worried about you, because I want you to be happy.'

'I won the art competition,' Douglas told him. 'I was coming home to tell Silverwing; I wanted him to know. Now it's too late!'

He cried again and this time his dad bent down beside him.

'No, Douglas, that's where you're wrong. Look what I found! Let's get inside and I'll read it to you.'

In the warm glow of the living room, they both sat on the sofa, close to each other. His dad pulled the red notebook out of his coat pocket, opened the last page and began to read aloud.

> *I went out early today because the geese were coming back from Iceland. They were flying over the house to go down to the valley, to the fields where they always spend the winter. And I knew for the first time my father wouldn't shoot them; he has promised never to shoot another goose. I went out to the back of the house and I was watching the sky – the geese were only twenty feet above my head. And then one landed in front of me, just a few feet away. It had a tiny white mark on its forehead, just like Littlewing. And all at once, I realised that it was Littlewing, that he had remembered and come back! It was as if he wanted me to know everything was all right. I knelt down and called his name, but he didn't come any closer – he just looked at me. I knew without a shadow of a doubt it was Littlewing, that it could only be him!*

As his dad finished reading, Douglas, snuggled warm against him, looked up at his face. That was the end of the book, the very last page. Douglas hadn't thought to look at the end, past the blank pages in the notebook. Maybe that was why the notebook had been left in the old house, the last place that his mum had seen Littlewing?

'That's why you can't give up hope, Douglas! I believe your mum wanted you to find this notebook, just as I believe she

wanted you to draw Silverwing! Look at all that's happened –
I don't believe any of it has been an accident! And I really
believe Silverwing may come back, just like your mum's goose.
You have to believe that, son!'

Douglas looked at his dad's excited face and he nodded.

'Can we go back to the old house sometimes?' he asked
softly. 'I feel Mum there, somehow more than in the village. I
love it up there.'

John nodded. 'I do too. Yes, we'll go back, maybe during
the summer? How about that? We could even spend the
holidays there.'

'And when the geese come back?' Douglas asked, his voice
even softer.

'Yes.' His dad smiled. 'And when the geese come back.'

ACTIVITY PAGES

WE HAVE LEFT YOU SOME BLANK PAGES TO DRAW OR TAKE NOTES ON AND RECORD NATURE LIKE DOUGLAS DOES. THERE ARE SOME IDEAS YOU CAN FOLLOW OR JUST DO YOUR OWN THING.

Can you name any of the islands or draw some of the lochs, mountains, or cities on this map of Scotland?

Douglas lives on the West coast of Scotland in an area called Argyll

If you don't live in Scotland, you could draw or write about your country and where you and your family and friends live.

Next time you are outside look for a
feather and a leaf that you like and then
draw them, or trace around their shape.
You could label your drawing with where
you found it and what type of bird, or tree,
it is from.

Try sitting quietly at the window for a few
minutes at different times of the day
and keep a record - in pictures or words - of any
birds or animals you see.

Douglas lives near the coast. Some animals he might spot from the shore include seals, otters, porpoises and dolphins. He might even catch the occasional glimpse of a shark or a whale!

Can you name or draw any sea animals or things you might find on the shore in Scotland or near where you live?

Have you ever seen a greylag goose? Or any of the other animals that Douglas and his Dad talk about?

 Maybe you could write your own story about meeting some of these animals.